T0381443

A Lesson Learned

CATHRYN EDELMAN

BALBOA.PRESS
A DIVISION OF HAY HOUSE

Balboa Press books may be ordered through booksellers or by contacting:

Balboa Press
A Division of Hay House
1663 Liberty Drive
Bloomington, IN 47403
www.balboapress.com
844-682-1282

Because of the dynamic nature of the Internet, any web addresses or links contained in this book may have changed since publication and may no longer be valid. The views expressed in this work are solely those of the author and do not necessarily reflect the views of the publisher, and the publisher hereby disclaims any responsibility for them.

The author of this book does not dispense medical advice or prescribe the use of any technique as a form of treatment for physical, emotional, or medical problems without the advice of a physician, either directly or indirectly. The intent of the author is only to offer information of a general nature to help you in your quest for emotional and spiritual well-being. In the event you use any of the information in this book for yourself, which is your constitutional right, the author and the publisher assume no responsibility for your actions.

Any people depicted in stock imagery provided by Getty Images are models, and such images are being used for illustrative purposes only. Certain stock imagery © Getty Images.

Print information available on the last page.

ISBN: 979-8-7652-3292-7 (sc)
ISBN: 979-8-7652-3293-4 (e)

Balboa Press rev. date: 09/05/2022

Gratitude

I am grateful to my husband Alan for supporting in my writing endeavors and having to listen to long hours of brainstorming ideas to get my story "just right". I am also grateful for my friends Adrianna Basa, Shannon Brooke, and Lynette Lockett for their encouragement when I was discouraged with my writing. Thank you for believing in me everyone. I couldn't have done this without you!

CONTENTS

September

A S SHE PULLED up to the curb and turned off the engine, she grips the wheel, not wanting to go inside. It's only the second week of September, but for the millionth time this year, Daniella Ellis regrets staying at this school. The pretty 5'4 Caucasian looks in her mirror on the inside of her visor and fixes her shoulder length brown hair, brushing it back behind her ears. She tells herself that she doesn't care if she would lose her tenure and have to start over, some jobs are just not worth it. She is so tired of all the adversarial moments at this school. No one seems to care.

In the last four years that she has been at this school, there have been several teachers hurt, the parents and the students have virtually taken over the school to the point the teachers are afraid and can't do their jobs, and no one wants to teach here. There has been a higher teacher turnover rate at this school then at all the other schools in the district combined. There are never enough textbooks, or even paper and pencils. Fights break out almost every day and the list continued to grow. The worst part of this whole situation is that there are NEVER any consequences for any student breaking a school rule. Seagrove Elementary is just not safe.

She could move school sites, put in a transfer request directly to HR. She has tried several times the last couple of years through the principal, per the policy, however, she has yet to hear anything.

District office does not seem to care what is happening down here at this school. It seems like a lawsuit just waiting to happen. Although the injuries were all considered to be minor injuries, the administration seemed to try to cover them up. They did eventually get out through rumors; however, Daniella is beginning to wonder if there is truth in those rumors.

The parents pretty much run the school now. They come in and tell the principal what they want and most of the time he does it. One such example is two years ago, the textbook fund that was supposed to buy the first grade updated math books since there were not enough and the old ones were falling apart. Several of the books had missing covers, or missing pages, or both. The parents never saw the textbooks because they didn't go home and they said the teachers could simply make copies of the good textbooks. The parents were more upset that they were being asked to send items for the holiday parties and told the principal to sponsor the holiday parties which he did. After fronting the money for the parties, there was $13 left in the textbook fund. According to his secretary, the ledger reads "educational materials".

This school, if it could be called that, had some major problems. In addition to the lack of materials, fights break out almost every day, but the principal says that "kids will be kids", New teachers constantly quit after just two to three months, there are never enough substitute teachers, and the list just goes on. The worst part of it is that there are no consequences *ever* for any student for any infraction. This school is just not a safe school environment for anyone who enters, yet it never seems to get better.

Daniella slowly let go of the wheel, takes a few deep breaths and exits the car. She is behind her car taking out her blue crate with the handle and wheels when she heard the familiar, always screaming, high pitched voice. She tried desperately to pretend that she had not heard it while she lifts the crate to the ground.

"Mizz Ellis!"

The voice is beginning to grow louder now and again Daniella tries to look lost in her own thoughts. It's only 7:15 she thinks, why do there have to be parents here this early? She begins to wonder if it's too early in the year to take a sick day. She slowly makes her way to the front of the building, towards the screaming voice. Trying to look oblivious to the world, she is holding her free hand just below her face as if she is calculating something on her fingers.

"Mizz Ellis!" Goodness this mom surely had a knack for hitting some high pitches!

"Good Morning Miss Foley." Daniella tries to put on her most pleasant and professional voice. It is only the first three weeks of school and she already knew this parent by name.

"When you gonna schedule those field trips? It's already into the school year and pretty soon y'alls gonna be tellin' us it's too late for field trips! My baby gots to go on them trips! He's been waitin!"

Why can this woman not talk in a normal tone?

"I am so sorry. I am just arriving and I haven't checked my box since our discussion yesterday after school to see if anything new has arrived. I have put out several requests and now I am waiting on the responses. It *is* only the third week of school and we *did* have a holiday which does have a tendency to slow people down in getting back to us. However, I do have on my notes for this week to start making calls to check in. I wouldn't mind a parent volunteer to help me make those calls, if of course you have the time......." Daniella smiles sweetly at the irate woman.

"Good Lord lady! I ain't gonna do your job fur ya!"

"How did Josiah do on his homework last night?" Daniella changes the subject quickly before she has to listen again to this woman's lecture of what her job is. This seems to be Ms. Foley's favorite pastime.

"You one crazy teacher givin' him work that's too hard for him to do. I just tolds him don't do it. That was way too hard for him. What you gotta make him trace letters for anyway and practice words like 'at' and 'cat'. My baby can read and write! He smarter than anybody! Mr. Griggs says we gonna move him up to second grade soon but he still gonna do all the fun stuff you do. Oh and why you not giving my Joshy any food? He tells me you said they gotta bring snacks from home. I ain't got food to spare to send to school. You 'posed to be feeding dem while dey at school. That's why we filled dem papers for free food out right? Why ain't dey getting der food?"

"I *am* sorry Ms. Foley. I have asked for donations for snack time but have not received any. We will have the fresh fruit program again this year starting the first week in October. Our designated day will be Thursdays. Then I can promise every Thursday everyone will have something. The papers you filled out was for free breakfast and lunches from the cafeteria, not snacks from the classrooms. I think the cafeteria might be open already if you would like to head over there." Daniela knew full well that the cafeteria didn't open for another 15 minutes but she was hoping to distract the short, stocky, African American mom for at least a few minutes so she could get to her room to start setting up for the day. No such luck.

"Den you gots to go to de sto! My baby gots to eat!"

"I'm sorry Mrs. Foley, I am not able to that."

"It's yo job!" Daniella really hated that the parents had absolutely no clue what her job really was. It seems *none* of the parents had a clue and they tried to boss around the teachers all the time.

"I'm sorry Ms. Foley, it is not. I really need to get inside and get set up for the day. Have a good day." Daniella knew she had gotten a bit assertive in her tone but she really needed to break this off. She turns and walks into the building with Ms. Foley and her son standing outside. She could her the woman muttering under her breath that the white bitch really didn't know her job.

Daniella quickly enters the main office, looks around and breathes a giant sigh of relief. No sign of Mr. Griggs. The less of that man she sees, the better. She quickly signs in, checks her box, and heads to her room. Daniella had been in her classroom for about 20 minutes when she heard the sound of a key in the door lock. As the door opens, in walks Mr. Griggs, looking like he has just been whipped like a disobedient school boy. *Great! What does he want!*

Feeling a bit apprehensive, she turns to face him as tries to convince herself not to panic. He walks up to one of the small desks, plays with an already torn name tag for a minute then sits on the edge of the small desk, partially hanging off.

"Miss Ellis, I just had an interesting meeting with one of your parents this morning. Ms. Foley feels that you don't care about her son and that are not listening to her concerns. The one thing we need to do is to keep parents happy. If the parents are happy, then the students will be happy and will learn better. After all that is what we want right? So, if the parents want field trips, we organize field trips, if they want their kids to have snacks, we provide snacks, get it?" Without waiting for a response, he continues, "Now organizing a field trip is really not that hard. You can do it in a day. So, organize a field trip for next week. Stop by the store on your way home and pick up some crackers or chips or something. Something simple. It really is very easy you know."

"Mr. Griggs, you specifically told us in last week's staff meeting not to plan any field trips before October 13. Also, ..."

Mr. Griggs jumps in irritated, "I never said that!"

"Um, actually you did," Daniella walks over to her file cabinet, opens a drawer and pulls out a folder. "'Here is a copy of the Agenda provided by your assistant. Right here," Daniella points to the line "it says no field trips before October 13."

"It's fine. We will work around it." He sighs as he gets up to go.

"Also, I have requested tech support to come and help with the computer in my room and they said they are still waiting for your approval. I still do not have internet access or email since getting hacked last year. I cannot work on any field trips without this."

"Then you need to submit the request form."

"I gave it to you twice last year and the first week of school this year."

"Well I never got it so you will have to redo it. You can use your home computer to set things up in the meantime. You don't have to do it here."

"Mr. Griggs, I handed you the paperwork and you cannot tell me I have to work at home or spend my own money to buy snacks for the kids."

"Miss Ellis, do you really have to fight about everything? Why can't you just say ok just once? Just organize a field trip for next week." He sighed and started to walk out of the room.

"It takes quite a bit of time to organize a field trip. I have to find a place and time, organize chaperones, file all the insurance forms with the district which generally takes about two to three weeks, and get permission slips from the parents, not to mention figure out how we will get there and back."

"That's just paperwork. Just get the permission slips and go. The rest you can catch up later. It will be fine." He says as he walks out the door.

Daniella shakes her head. As she resumes getting ready for the day, she once again wonders about the district level supervisors. *How does the district think so highly of him? What is the missing link here?* She sighs. *I don't have the energy or the desire to figure it out. I need to find a new job. Fast.*

This was just one more reason for Daniella to hate her principal. Over the last three years of working here, she has grown to hate him more and more for conversations and put downs just like what had just happened. Sometimes worse. She was just waiting to reach tenure so she could put in for a transfer. Fortunately, she obtained tenure last year. However, she had to put her transfer request in through Mr. Griggs. She reached tenure on the first day of school. She gave her transfer request to Mr. Griggs on October 1. At the Thanksgiving break she had not heard anything so she asked the principal about her transfer. His response was that he didn't have the paperwork. She resubmitted it the next day. After the winter break holidays, she called the district office to inquire. They said they still did not have it. She again asked Mr. Griggs who said because of the holidays, he said he hadn't had the time to look at it. She waited two weeks and asked again. This time the principal tried to talk her out of the transfer by saying there was only a couple of months left of school why not wait until the end of the year. she agreed for the sake of the children to not have a new teacher in the middle of the Year.

At the end of the year she had put her paperwork in to Mr. Griggs on the last day of April. When she had not heard from the district by the beginning of August, she called them. They did not have any paperwork for her. She contacted Mr. Griggs who much to her dismay, told her he had rejected her request because he needed her there. At this point she realizes that he will never sign a transfer for her and she will have to take much more drastic actions. She contacted her union rep who told her that they would look into it. When they got back to her, she was told that she was to try this year if she still wanted it, and to rimacedt everything. She was to try three times and then she could put it in directly to the HR dept. She was to copy everything to her union rep. She just filed the first paperwork of the year for the transfer last week and had to give two weeks for a response.

As soon as Daniella opens her door for her students, Ms. Foley is standing there with a smug look on her face.

"Mr. Griggs says yous gonna do a field trip next week and yous gonna give dem snacks every day. He was ways more nicer dan you. If yous just doos what I tells yous, yous wouldn't make me go to gets him and you wouldn't gets in no trouble."

Daniella ignores the taunts from Ms. Foley and turns her attention to her students. On each of the desks is the daily warm-up and as students are coming in Daniella is circulating with reminders about the morning routines. When the bell rings, Daniella calls everyone to the carpet. She is still very aware Ms. Foley is still in the room, however, she chooses to not engage and starts the day.

About five minutes later a very grumpy Ms. Foley leaves the room. Daniella smiles to herself that she was able to keep her professionalism intact and continues with the morning lesson.

Later, after a rough morning of noncompliance and disrespect from her students, she walks the class to the cafeteria. Once she ensures that everyone has lunch and is settled, she walked back to the classroom feeling the emergence of a stress related headache. She commonly ate her lunch while she worked because she didn't want to have to stay 1 minute longer after school than what was necessary by contract.

Suddenly there was a knock at the door. She looked up and felt a wave of relief to see her friend, Courtney Mosely at the door.

Courtney was a sweet 5'2 beautiful skinny blond who radiated friendship. It seemed like everyone on the staff loved her and she liked them all, except of course the principal. She found it difficult to follow some of his rules as he would contradict them the very next day. Courtney taught Kindergarten down the hall so when she joined the staff two years ago and the Kindergarten and first grade teachers tried to work together to unify the younger grades, Courtney and Daniella became fast friends.

Although this would be Courtney's third year on the team, she had already decided to look for another job. She had just secretly redone her resume and was sending it out the next week. She had only told Daniella and Daniella might be doing the same. She needed to talk to her husband first.

"Hey!" Daniella says opening the door which she always kept locked.

"How was your morning......" began Courtney. She stopped suddenly when she saw her friend's face.

"The usual garbage from Griggs. You?"

"Yeah me too. The kindergarten parents are convinced that I am not teaching their children correctly because they are not reading chapter books yet. It's only the second freaking month of the year. I hope I find a job soon. I was going to send out those resumes on Monday, I might do it tomorrow!"

Daniella told her about the exchange before school.

"Oh my gosh! What are you going to do?"

"I'm going to call the union rep tonight. He cannot require us to do certain things simply because the parents want it."

"I agree. I am going to make an appointment in HR for next week. I decided to resign. I am not going to wait until I find another job. I have enough in savings to last the rest of the year if necessary and I can always sub in other districts. I have had enough. Tyronne and Leon got into another fight and Mr. Griggs let them play in the computer lab until they started fighting in there and then he sent one to the Library."

"Wow, so if you fight you don't get sent home or even have your parents called, instead you are rewarded with play time. Unbelievable. I want to resign too but I need to talk to the hubby first. We are really tight financially right now."

Just then the bell rang "Great!" said Courtney said with dread in her voice, "here we go again." The two quickly went their separate ways to collect their classes and see what has unfolded during lunch.

That afternoon at home, Daniella calls the union representative who assures her he will have the principal on the phone no later than tomorrow morning or he will show up that afternoon at the school. After the conversation, Daniella returns her attention to the kids and getting homework done. Then she starts her evening routine and begins dinner.

When her husband walks in he smells something burning. He immediately goes to the kitchen where he sees a very distracted Daniella absentmindedly poking what used to be some kind of meat.

"Daniella!" His voice makes her jump. She looks down and starts to cry. She turns off the heat and puts the pan in the sink running water in a now steaming pan.

"Honey, don't cry. We'll order pizza. The kids will love it because it's the middle of the week and we are treating it like a weekend. Here let me get changed and I'll help."

When Jack came back now wearing sweats and t-shirt, he started working on the burnt remains in the pan while Daniella cleaned the stove and put things away. While they worked, she told him about the morning's events.

"How bad do still want to work there?" Jack asks her.

"Well, I finally have tenure and I can go over Mr. Griggs head and request a transfer. Besides I know we are tight right now and I can't be without a job."

"Whatever you decide I will support you and don't worry about money. We will make it work."

"I know." She replies as she starts crying again.

"Right now I want you to try to forget about the day, go in the bathroom, put on some relaxing music and take a hot bath. I will deal with the kids tonight."

Just then the doorbell rang and the pizza had arrived. Daniella headed into the other room as she thought about how amazing her husband was. He has listened so many nights since she started working there.

The next day, Daniella was sitting at her desk during lunch, grading papers when she remembered she hadn't made the copies of the activity she wanted to do that afternoon. So she grabbed the original and went to the copy room.

When she got back there was a pile of snacks of all kinds with a note attached to one of the boxes of snacks: "For your students -Mr. G".

Later that afternoon she found a note in her box. "Take your time scheduling a field trip but try to do one in the next couple of months. Let me know if you need help – Mr. G." *Wow*, Daniella thought, *Union rep was true to his word,*

A week later, Daniella is just about to leave for the day when Courtney knocks on her door in tears. Daniella opens her door for her friend and asks her what happened.

"Last week Tyronne's dad came in and said the homework was too hard. I needed to send home easier homework. I tried to explain that identifying shapes and basic patterns was the beginning of reading and math and it was a skill that would be practiced all year and then built upon in the other grades, so it was crucial to Kindergarten. He yelled at me that I needed to learn how to do my job and left. His mom yells at me at least twice a week about his constant fighting. They are both are convinced I don't know how to teach or have any classroom management skills. Last Friday, they both came in to see Mr. Griggs and today he came in during class and reprimanded me in front of my class because I didn't have control of my class. About 40 minutes ago Tyronne's dad came in and said if I don't learn how to control the kids and give better homework I would be very sorry. I tried to stay calm and offered to work with his son during one recess a day and he yelled at me saying that if I couldn't teach him while I was in class with him, what made him think I could teach during a recess? He said people like me often end up getting hurt if they continue to be "racist bitches"." She put the emphasis on the last part and started crying.

"Did you report this?"

"Mr. Griggs said I just didn't get the climate of the school. Listen to what the dad says because he knows his son better than I do. He is just angry. He will calm down and I need to calm myself down."

"Unfreaking believable! This is a threat. We need to report this. You are coming home with me."

The two girls walk towards the front of the building when Mr. Griggs approaches them. Not even addressing Daniella he says, "Ms. Mosely, you shouldn't give homework to your students. They are just babies. This may be why your test scores have always been low. You are exhausting your students." He walks away before either of the girls can respond.

As the ladies walk out of the building they hear Tyronne's father yell at them from across the street.

"Hey Bitch! You pick on my son again and I'll pop you one! You will regret ever coming here! You're no teacher! You're just a lazy, ..."

"Courtney, get in the car!" The low controlled command came from Daniella who saw Courtney frozen in place. Courtney got in the car and the two rode the 20 minutes to Daniella's home in silence.

Once they were at Daniella's home, Courtney finally broke. She started crying and then apologizing, "I am so sorry I dragged you into my mess, you must be furious...."

Daniella jumped in, "I am furious but not at you. I am furious at Mr. Griggs for allowing this. I am furious at this father. Who does he think he is?" She reaches for her cell phone and brings up a contact and dials.

"Honey, I am so sorry to ask this but can you leave right now and get the kids and get home?" She continued by telling him what had happened.

"I want you to call the police immediately! Did he follow you?"

"No. We are safe."

"Good. I am leaving right now."

After hanging up with her husband, Daniella called Union Rep, Ramon Miles who said he was on his way over and to call the police out.

Just 30 minutes later, with her husband already home and Ramon there, Courtney and Daniella are describing for the police the events of the afternoon and the history of events leading up to this.

The next morning as the two ladies head towards the building, they notice the squad car out front. When they enter the office to sign in, Mr. Griggs sees them.

"Here they are now. Ms. Ellis, Ms. Mosely would you come in here please." As Mr. Griggs introduces Officer Marsh, whom Daniella recognizes as the school resource officer, Mr. Griggs continues, "I am so sorry that they have wasted your time. These two ladies are a bit ultra-sensitive and take every harsh word as a threat. I will be advising them to seek professional help through district resources. They don't really want to press charges against a parent who simply upset, they just overreacted and I will remind them about the consequences of their actions."

The officer stood up, shook Mr. Griggs hand, "Thanks for clearing this up. I'll close the case."

Daniella was outraged. "Of course we want to press charges!"

Officer Marsh looked at her for a moment and shook his head. He said, "Thank you for your time, Mr. Griggs. Ladies." With that he walked out. Mr. Griggs watched him go then turned to Courtney.

"You need to get yourself together. If every time a parent is upset with you, you take it as a threat, then maybe you should think about a different career. This is not basket weaving. Perhaps you need a break. Let's consider a leave for you to think about things. Let's talk later this week about this."

Courtney leaves and as Daniella is fuming and thinking her next move, she gets up to follow her. Mr. Griggs stops her. "Be careful who you are friends with. She is emotional and overreacts. Do not get pulled in.

She could wreck your career along with hers. Talk to her, calm her down. Perhaps, end your friendship with her. For both of you."

He walked out before she could respond. She could think of a few choice words for him, but…..

A couple of days later, the ladies were eating lunch in Courtney's room and Daniella was helping her to hang some of the children's work when the bell rang. As the ladies headed out to collect the classes, Myisha and Nicole ran up to them.

"Tyronne and Dalton got in a fight! There is blood everywhere!" Myisha reports. Dalton was a second grader in Edna's class. Why was he even out with the K-1 group, Daniella wonders as she listens.

"They took him to the office." Adds Nicole.

Well at least Courtney will have a break for a little bit this afternoon with Tyronne out of the room.

About an hour and a half later, an announcement is made over the intercom. "Mr. Farmer, please come to room 5." *This was the emergency code! Room 5! That's Courtney's room!* Silent panic begins to build in Danielle as she closes and locks her doors, checks her windows, lower the blinds and turns off the lights. She quickly calls all the students away from the doors and windows to a small carpet in the partially self – contained cubby area and begins a quiet game. She tries to remain calm, but all she wants to do is run to Courtney's room.

After what seems an eternity, the all clear announcement comes. Since the students missed their recess, Daniela decided to take them out for a late recess. While she was outside with the students, Mr. Griggs came out to talk to her.

"I need you to take care of Ms. Mosely's purse. Can you take it to her? She is at Mercy General."

"Oh my gosh! Is she alright? What happened?"

"She is fine. She just had a small accident. Kindergarten was over for the day so we just put the other students who hadn't been picked up yet in a different room."

He walked away from her as this was absolutely normal. Now Daniela was in a near panic. Her friend was hurt and the principal acts as if nothing is wrong.

As the day ends, Daniella grabs her own purse and heads to Courtney's classroom. She always keeps her purse in the bottom drawer of the file cabinet. As she enters the room she sees large amounts of blood and chairs and desks strewn about everywhere. Daniella grabs her phone and takes about a dozen pictures of the room. She is not quite sure why but she feels that these may come in handy very soon.

As she is walking out, Madelyn the fourth grade teacher enters. "Hi, how is Courtney?"

"Hi. I haven't heard. I'm going to the hospital now. I have her purse."

Madelyn looked uncomfortable then walked out into the hall, looked around and came back in shutting the door. "You didn't hear this from me. I only caught part of what was going on. Tyronne's dad was in here. He was yelling something about his split lip. He was saying something about her not doing her job. He was really mad, then he started throwing chairs and desks around. I'm not sure what happened, but I don't think it was her fault." With that Madelyn looked out in the hallway again and anxiously bowed her head and left.

Daniella headed straight out of the school and to her car. She raced the 15 minutes to Mercy General praying she wouldn't get a ticket. As she headed into the hospital, she called the union rep again. He said he would meet her at the hospital in 20 minutes. She then called her husband. He said he would ask his mom to pick up the kids and then he would be on his way to the hospital.

Daniella quickly found her friends room and went in. She was very relieved to find her sitting up in bed, however the damage to her face and all the bandages on her arms frightened Daniella. "How do you feel?"

"Except for the pounding headache?" Courtney tried to laugh but it sounded hollow.

Just then the union rep, Roman walked in and rimaced. "Hey, how do you feel?"

She repeated that she had a bad headache. "I have a broken nose, some broken facial bones, broken ribs, a broken wrist. The doctor is worried that I may need reconstructive surgery but only time will tell."

Daniella was near tears but knew she had to be strong. "Ramon, I think you better see these." With that she pulled out her phone and showed him the pictures of the classroom.

"That was great you took pictures. Can you send me those?"

"Yes."

"Great. Ok Courtney, I hate to do this but I am gonna have to ask you what happened. Do you want Daniella to leave?"

"No I would like her here."

"Ok, so can you start from the top?"

"I was with Daniella at lunchtime in my room hanging some papers, when Myisha and Nicole came in and said Tyronne and a kid from the fourth grade got in another fight. Tyronne had a split lip and was in the office. I think he needed stitches. I picked up my class after lunch and taught the rest of the day, pretty much without any challenges other than the normal ones and when the bell rang I went over and opened my door. Parents were already lining up, so I started calling student names to release them. I saw Tyronne's dad and he walked up to me and pushed me backwards into the room. I lost my balance and fell against one of the bookshelves. He started yelling at me about not doing my job and how come I didn't protect his son. I tried to explain that I was not out there at lunch and he said I was not where I was supposed to be. He was swearing a lot, kicking chairs and desks. I asked him to stop or I would call the office. He continued to yell at me the whole time. Then he picked up a chair and threw it at me. I couldn't get away fast enough. It hit me in the back of the head because I turned to protect my face. I fell from the hit because it was so hard. Then he jumped on top of me and started hitting me everywhere. Next thing I know I was waking up here."

"Geez. Did you get to call the office?"

"No, I didn't reach the phone in time."

"Did you have any warning prior to today that this parent would get physical?"

"Yes and I told Mr. Griggs that I was uncomfortable. There was a situation with this particular parent making a threat that I reported to both Mr. Griggs and the police, but Mr. Griggs told the school resource officer that I was overreacting and retracted the report. I was then placed on report with the school district for not following proper channels. I think you were helping me on that one. It was finally retracted."

"That's right, I remember that one. Did you know that this parent was upset before you saw him?

"No, I was calling kids and suddenly he was there."

"I hate to have to do this, but I need to take some pictures of your injuries."

"Ok. Who will see them?"

"For now only us and the principal. However, I may have to take this further up the chain but I will do my best to only show them to whom I must."

"Ok." Ramon then took the pictures with his phone.

"Ok, I think I have everything, for now I would like you to get some rest. I will visit again soon."

"Thanks."

Daniella had been silent the entire time Courtney was talking. Now she couldn't help it. "Oh Courtney!" Tears started flowing. Just then Jack walks in and hugs Daniella and gives Courtney a gentle hug to avoid hurting her.

"Courtney, how do you feel?"

"I'm feel like I look, but the doctors are hopeful."

"Good. When you get out of here, you can stay with us as long as you need to."

"Thank you."

They visit for about another 30 minutes and then both Jack and Daniella gave Courtney one more gentle squeeze hug and said their goodbyes. Daniella promised to visit the next day after school.

The Monday after Courtney had gotten hurt was the scheduled staff meeting. Most of the staff knew she had gotten hurt somehow but didn't know the particulars, and only a couple of teachers knew that a parent had been involved. No one except Daniella and Mr. Griggs knew everything.

Mr. Griggs opened the staff meeting with this announcement. "I know many of you know that Ms. Mosely has gotten hurt and is not here right now."

Oh, this is going to be rich, thought Daniella. She didn't know quite what made her do it, but she pushed the record button on her phone. She looked over and saw that two other teachers were doing the same thing. *Hmmmm*, she thought. *Mr. Griggs might be in more trouble than he realizes.*

"Ms. Mosely was doing something she knew she shouldn't do and was hurt in the process. My understanding is that she was trying to move some of the larger bookshelves in her room and in the process one fell on her. Fortunately, one of our male parents was nearby and was able to come to her aid. It is unknown at this time, if ever, she will be returning to Brookside. Let this be a warning to all of you. If you need something done you are not supposed to do, let's talk and do it through the proper channels."

As the meeting moved on to other topics, Daniella pushed the stop button and sat in stunned silence. She missed most of the rest of the meeting because she absolutely appalled at what Mr. Griggs had said. He just shouldered all the blame on Courtney! He flat out lied! How dare he!

After the meeting Mr. Griggs had gone off to his office and several teachers approached her wanting to know if that was what really happened. Daniella knew better than to say anything at work so she simply announced loudly, "There will be a potluck at my house tonight at 6:00pm."

Everyone knew why and nodded their heads.

Daniella went to her classroom, gathered her belongings and went to the office. Once in the office, she spoke with Ms. Johnson, the secretary to Mr. Griggs. "I would like to make an appointment with Mr. Griggs tomorrow for myself and my union rep."

The gray haired lady looked up and smiled kindly at her. "I understand dear. He will want to know the reason."

"Of course. My union rep and I will need to talk to him about today's staff meeting."

"Yes, of course." Mrs. Johnson scheduled the appointment for 7am so that they would have time before school started.

Daniella thanked her and started towards her car to drive home.

"Mizz Ellis!"

Oh, God!, thought Daniella. She turned around and there was Ms. Foley. She was so tired of this parent and how she was bullying her she decided to record it and pushed the button on her phone in her pocket.

"We all heard 'bout your teacher friend. We want you and the other teachers to know that we ain't playin' when it comes to our kids. You bets be watching yoself!"

With that she humphed and walked away, leaving Daniella with no opportunity to respond.

Daniella still in disbelief climbs into her car and turns off the recording. She puts her phone on the speaker and calls her union rep while she is driving. She explained what had happened at the meeting and that several teachers were questioning her but she didn't know what she could tell them. They were coming over to her place that night for a potluck. Her union rep said that he would be there as well. She replied her thanks and also told him of Ms. Foley's threats and that she had recorded it.

That night everyone was gathering at Daniella's house. Fortunately the union rep took the lead. He explained what he could about what really happened, where Courtney really was and how to visit if they wanted to. He warned that none of them should meet alone with Mr. Griggs without having the union rep there. He was going to file a list of complaints against Mr. Griggs by Friday if he didn't have some solutions by then. He and Daniella were meeting with Mr. Griggs in the morning. He advised against talking about any of the current situations at the school on campus. He said they should come directly to him with concerns that Mr. Griggs is not handling.

Although everyone was tense at these developments they all agreed and decided that since Daniella's house was most central that they could meet there once a week to document and devise a plan to make the school safer. The teachers started leaving and although no one felt any relief, they did acknowledge that it felt better to be trying to do something.

The next morning, Ramon and Daniella arrived at the school and tried to meet with Mr. Griggs. He called them into his office and had Daniella's personnel file on the table. He apologized to the union rep citing that Daniella was a troublemaker and that her file contained all the write-ups she has had in the last three years. "She is merely retaliating. I was considering a transfer for her. In fact, I have another write-up here that I am glad you are here to see. It is for being late every day for the last two weeks. Also for unprofessional behavior with a parent."

Daniella was outraged. "What write-ups! I haven't had one! Show me! And I have been begging for a transfer. I will not sign the phony write up you are trying to give me now!"

"Ms. Ellis, you have a copy of every one, they were signed by you." Replied Mr. Griggs.

Ramon put his hand on Daniella's arm and she quieted her protests. "Mr. Griggs, could I get a copy of those please?"

"Of course." He walks to the outer office.

"Let me get the copies. I'll come over tonight." He whispers.

Mr. Griggs comes back into the inner office. "Ms. Ellis, you have until tomorrow morning to sign the write up for today or you will be placed on administrative leave. Is there anything else?"

Ramon speaks up, "Actually there is. I have a list of complaints made by several staff members I would like you to look at then respond to me by noon on Friday with regards to each complaint."

"Yeah, ok." Mr. Griggs takes the paper and tosses it on the table.

"Now, I need to go unlock the gates for students to come in." He didn't wait for a response but strode out of the door.

Ramon and Daniella looked at each other. They nodded at one another and went separate ways at the office door. Ramon retrieved the copies from the secretary and Daniella went to her classroom.

That night, Ramon came over and showed Daniella and Jack the write-ups. Daniella was the first to speak. "These are totally fake! That's not even my signature!"

"I suspected as much by your reaction today and that was why I stopped you. I need several samples of your writing preferably your signature."

"Of course. I'll be right back." Daniella went to the office and came back with some papers. "I have a few cancelled checks and a letter I wrote to Jack while we were dating, I was on vacation with some friends, and I have my teaching contract."

"Those are perfect. I will make copies and make sure you get them back. I will go to HR tomorrow to have these write-ups pulled. Also do not sign this new one."

The next morning, Mr. Griggs came and spoke to Daniella. "I want to give you a chance to redeem yourself so I tore up your write up." Then without another word he turned and walked out of the room. Daniella could do nothing but stare after him in disbelief. Then she grabbed her phone and texted Ramon what had just happened.

The rest of the month was spent much the same as the beginning with parents yelling at teachers, telling them what to do, students getting out of hand etc. For Daniella it seemed to drag by, especially without Courtney there. She would need at least a month to recover and possibly reconstructive surgery which would put her out even longer.

Daniella did start making a better friendship with Madelyn, the fourth grade teacher. After what had happened to Courtney, Madelyn was becoming afraid and confided in Daniella.

One day near the end of September, Madelyn came to Daniella's room at the end of the school day. "I hate to impose…...can I come over to your house after school today?"

"Of course! Are you ok?"

"No …we can talk later." She starts to sniffle like she is about to cry but then collects herself and walks away.

Later that evening, Madelyn and Daniella are sitting on Daniella's couch sipping tea.

Madelyn starts slowly. "I saw the trouble in some of the classrooms and found myself very thankful I had only some minor challenges. I mean that I have some of the boys that get out of hand from time to time, but it's nothing compared to the rest of you, then today…….." her voice trailed off as she held back her tears.

Daniella leaned towards her and put her hand over Madelyn's. "What happened?"

"After recess this morning, Judy came to me and was crying and scared. She said that Dante had threatened her with a knife. When I asked him about it in class he got defensive. I asked if he had a knife and he pulled it from his pants and flipped it open. I immediately hit the emergency code on the phone and Mr. Griggs came to the classroom. He walked in looked around and saw Dante with the knife and walked out. Dante was screaming something about the school and that he wouldn't let the school do to him what they had done to his brother and waving the knife around. I finally was able to calm him down and get the knife and send my students to other classrooms. I then walked him down to the office and handed the knife to Mr. Griggs. He said thanks and that he would take it from there. I found out after school that he had given the knife back to the parents and there was no consequence!"

At this point, Madelyn started crying. "I'm not a weak teacher but that terrified me! Mr. Griggs said I didn't understand boys!"

Daniella was silent for a moment and then asked Madelyn if she would like to talk the union rep. Did she feel safe at school etc.

Madelyn looked at her and said, "Do you think I should?"

"Yes.", was all Daniella could reply. They called Roman and told him of what had happened and he said to write it all down and send it to him.

After Madelyn went home, Daniella talked to Jack.

"I'm going to start looking. It's getting worse. Parents can beat teachers up with no consequences, students can bring weapons, I don't feel safe and I can get a job at another school with a different district. You need to know I will lose my tenure and have to start over."

"Okay, let's do it. What do you need from me?"

They talked a while, worked out a plan and then went to bed.

October

IT'S BEEN A few weeks since Courtney was hurt by the angry parent. Mr. Griggs did his best to keep that information a secret but the parents did a great job spreading the news themselves and some of them were only to please to tell some of the teachers hinting at warning them. By the end of the first week she was out, all the teachers knew. All that Daniella would tell anyone was that the union was involved and that they should talk to Ramon.

It wasn't really a surprise but it did take Daniella a minute to process when Madelyn submitted her resignation. She was leaving immediately and Mr. Griggs who was meeting with her in his office could be heard in the outer office. "You will lose your tenure and you will be charged for the rest of the school year by HR for breaking your contract."

Madelyn somehow kept her composure and replied, "That is okay, I will deal with the repercussions. I cannot work like this."

Daniella was really sorry to see Madalyn go. She was a sweet teacher who really believed in what she was doing. She just stated that she could not work with a principal who gave weapons back to students. It only took her a week to find another job. While Daniella was happy for her, she also was slightly jealous. Courtney is thinking that when she is better she is not going back to teaching anymore. She is going to go back to the business world and finish her marketing degree. Daniella has just now decided to put her resume out. She is hoping to hear in the couple of weeks from when they go out.

Joshua Shaw came on board to take Madalyn's place as a fourth grade teacher. This tall, skinny, African-American Male thought that this would be a good school for him and that he could make a difference here because he grew up in the inner city. A person has to be strong to work in the inner city. Kids need tough love is the way his mom raised him. They need limits and they need consequences, something this school seems to be desperately missing.

As Joshua sets up for his class, he makes a mental note. He needs to have a meeting with Mr. Griggs. If things do not start to change in the immediate future, he will not stay. Of course, Joshua would honor his contract until the end of the year, that was his style, he would keep his word, however, if he were to stay in this district, he would ask for another school.

Joshua was writing the daily warm-up on the board when Jonathan, one of his quieter, more studious students, comes bursting through the door and out of breath. Joshua knows that it must be serious because although Jonathan is not a kid who causes trouble, he is also habitually late because he makes sure his little sister gets to her Kindergarten class. As Joshua turns around to tell Jonathan to slow down, the look on Jonathan's face stops him. There is a look of sheer terror.

Still out of breath, he exclaims, "Mr. Shaw! Mr. Shaw!"

Jonathan was not given to wild moments of panic, so Joshua actually felt some anxiousness rising up within his core being.

"Jonathan, slow down and tell me what is wrong."

"Mr. Shaw, Angelo says he is going to bring a gun to school! He is going to shoot all of us!"

"When did he say this?

"Just now! He's on the playground!"

"Okay, here is what we are going to do. Don't talk to anyone. Go directly to the office and wait for Mr. Griggs. If he is not there I want you to wait for him. I will go to the playground and see if I see him there. Okay?"

Sometimes Mr. Griggs could be found on the playground before school started and Joshua was hoping that today would be one of those days.

"Yes, sir." Jonathan ran out of the room and Joshua headed to the playground.

Sure enough Mr. Griggs was on the playground. Angelo was just a few feet away making gestures at other kids like he was shooting them. Mr. Griggs was just watching. As Joshua got closer, he could hear Angelo making threats. *Why doesn't Mr. Griggs do something?* Joshua thinks frustrated.

Joshua approaches Mr. Griggs and asks him, "You can hear the threats that Angelo is making right?"

"Mr. Shaw, don't panic. There is no need for alarm, he is just a boy. He is probably just playing cops and robbers. Didn't you play that as a boy?"

"Shouldn't you talk to him, maybe make sure? I sent Jonathan to the office to wait for you because he heard Angelo say that he is going to come to school and shoot up the school. He is terrified."

"Mr. Shaw, don't get our students all wound up about nothing. It is bad enough that we have teachers who overreact, we don't need them to scare our students. Do you need a day off? It can't be today though because I don't have any subs."

"We are not talking about taking a day off. We are talking about the safety of our school!"

"Mr. Shaw! Calm yourself! If it makes you feel better I will look into this!"

"Yes it will thank you!

Joshua walks off very angry at Mr. Griggs response. He goes to the office to check on Jonathan. "Hi Jonathan, I found Mr. Griggs and told him you were here. Just wait for him here okay?"

"Okay, Mr. Shaw."

Joshua goes back to his class and continues to get ready for the day, however now he is preoccupied and noticed that he just pulled the wrong copies off his desk to set up. He stops and sends Ramon an email from his personal account.

The bell rings and Joshua goes down to get his class. Mr. Griggs meets him at the line. "I've decided that the whole situation is blown way out of proportion and that if you are so concerned about this, you can talk to him yourself."

He walks off before Joshua can respond. Joshua stood for about a minute in disbelief. Then he took his class up to start the day. The morning was fairly quiet with only the usual disruptions. Then at recess, Joshua had supervision this week so he decided that he would use the opportunity to talk with Angelo.

As he released the class to the playground, he asked Angelo to stay back. "Angelo, I want to check in with you. How are you?"

"Okay." Angelo mutters and kicks the ground.

"Angelo, I have a report from someone else that you are planning to bring a gun to school. I can't take that lightly. You have people scared. Now would you like to talk to someone? I could ask for a school counselor so that everything you talk about is secret......"

'I don't need to talk to someone! You promised to protect me and you don't! You lied!"

Angelo runs off. *I will give him some space and check in later,* thinks Joshua. At the end of recess Joshua and the other teachers blow the whistles for the signal for the students to line up at their classes lineup spots. Joshua takes his class to his classroom and as they get settled, Joshua notices that Angelo has not returned. He calls the office. Moments later, Mr. Griggs walks in.

"Mr. Shaw, you should not have left the playground without all of your students. You should have reported this immediately."

"You may not reprimand me in front of my students. This conversation is over."

Mr. Griggs looked at him for a long moment and walked out. An hour later and Angelo had not been found. Mr. Griggs was still wandering the halls looking in all the rooms. As the kids were heading to the lunchroom, Joshua stopped by and suggested calling the police.

"Don't panic, Mr. Shaw. He's is probably just pouting somewhere. You know how sensitive he is. He will come out."

Just then the school resource officer walks through the door with Angelo in tow. "I found him wandering the streets about a mile from here. He said he wasn't coming back here so I figured he must have had a hard morning. So I told him we face that which bothers us."

"Another student reported that Angelo threatened to bring a gun to school and I confronted him." Reports Joshua.

"Mr. Shaw don't take up the good officer's time. Thank you officer, we will take it from here." Mr. Griggs looks down at Angelo. "Have you had a hard morning?" he asks. Angelo nods. Mr. Griggs takes out his wallet and says, "Look, I have the school credit card. Let's order a pizza and some soda and then you can relax in the library."

"What?!"

"Mr. Shaw, it's all about building relationship. Then you can talk to the kids. They have to trust you first."

Mr. Griggs walks away with Angelo.

Joshua goes back up to his room, shuts his door and calls his union representative, Ramon, who advises him to call District Office and file a complaint which Joshua did.

The next morning as Joshua is signing in, Mr. Griggs comes out of his office and says, "Mr. Shaw, since you are so concerned about this situation from yesterday, you need to search backpacks before leading your students to your classroom."

"I am not authorized as a teacher to do that! It has to be you!" It is too late, Mr. Griggs is already walking away. Daniella had overheard the whole exchange as did the third grade teacher, Amber as they were both taking papers out of box.

Later on the playground, Joshua is checking backpacks and finding nothing leads his class to the room.

As they settle into class, Angelo comes in late. He is stopped by Mr. Shaw.

"Good Morning Angelo, I need to see inside your backpack."

"Why?" Angelo challenges him.

"Mr. Griggs has me checking bags this morning."

"Oh." He reluctantly slips his backpack off his shoulders and opens it. Joshua peers inside and sees a large kitchen knife.

"I'm going to need to take that."

"I need it! The kids, they chase me and beat me up after school!"

Mr. Shaw calls the office and Mr. Griggs comes in. Mr. Shaw explains the situation and Mr. Griggs says, "So what do you want me to do about it?"

Mr. Shaw got so angry, he knew his face was turning red. He kept his voice low and walked over to Mr. Griggs. He turned to face him and so the students wouldn't see his face. "I would like you to act like a principal and take this young man to the office and take the knife away and call his parents to come get him. Suspend him for the day for bringing a weapon to school." Mr. Shaw had difficulty keeping his voice a whisper but he somehow managed it. He turned and went back to teaching the class.

Mr. Griggs stared in disbelief then escorted Angelo out of the room.

Later that day, Joshua packed up his belongings for the day and was locking the classroom door when Mr. Griggs came up to him. "Mr. Shaw, I need you to sign this." He thrusts a paper at Joshua.

As Joshua reads the paper, his anger rages once again. However, he remembered to be professional. "Mr. Griggs, you do not have the right to write me up without the opportunity to have my union representative present. Nor do you have the right to write me up for exercising a contractual right to have a student removed from my classroom for having a weapon. I will not sign that without union representation."

Mr. Griggs mumbled something and walked away.

The next morning, Joshua had an uneasy feeling as he walked towards the school building. He couldn't put his finger on it, but something felt wrong. He had talked to his union rep last night about the events of the day. That had to be it. Joshua dismissed the feeling and walked in to the building. In his box he discovered a copy of the write up from the day before and where his signature should have been were the words "employee refused to sign".

Joshua was enraged and walked silently to his classroom. Since he was at work early, he sat down at his desk and wrote a statement and then printed two copies. After school that day, he drove over to the school site where the union president worked and then drove to the district office. While at the district office, Joshua filed a formal complaint against Mr. Griggs. This was NOT how a principal should behave.

About a week later, Madelyn came to the school in hopes of finding Daniella. As she was headed to Daniella's room, she ran into Mr. Griggs. "Good Morning sir." She nodded.

"What are you doing here? If you are here to see someone you need to sign in to the office and get a visitors badge."

"I did and here is my badge. I am just picking up something from Daniella."

"What are you picking up? It better not be something that belongs to the school."

"No, it's personal. It's just her phone number."

"You could have just called her for that. You don't have to come to the school"

"I would have called her if I had her number." Madelyn replies, a bit annoyed at this moment.

"Fine. Don't be here too long. Your presence is inappropriate at this time."

"Yes sir!" replies Madelyn, as she thinks about how glad she is that she found another job.

Once she had arrived at Daniella's room she relaxed a bit. It was amazing how irritated that man could make someone. She knocked gently on Daniella's classroom door. Daniella opened the door and invited her in.

"Hello, I came to see if you could give me some phone numbers. I am filing a formal complaint against the school and I need to list witness that were present at various times."

"Of course!" Daniella replied. The two worked on the list of numbers for a few minutes when there came the sound Daniella hates the most. A key in the lock. Sure enough seconds later Mr. Griggs enters the room.

"Ladies. Okay, Ms. Stout. You should have her number by now and be leaving."

"Yes, I was just saying goodbye." She gives Daniella a hug and whispers, "I'll call you tonight for the rest."

"Awww so touching." Mr. Griggs snears.

Madlyn walks past him without a word. Daniella stares at him with disbelief.

"Ms. Ellis, you seem to have quite a few friends around here. Please remember this is not a social club or a place to make friends. You are here to teach. You might want to try it sometime."

With that he walked out of the classroom leaving a fuming Daniella behind.

A few weeks later brought Halloween. That meant candy and costumes and behavior that was more outrageous than the usual craziness of the school. Daniella had sent out her usual note asking that healthy snacks rather than Candy be brought and no masks or weapons with the costumes please.

Sure enough the next morning, Ms. Foley was waiting for her. "Ms. Ellis! What right you got to be tellin us how to dress our kids and what to feed them?"

"Good morning Ms. Foley. Would you like to join me as I walk to the classroom?"

"I sure wood!"

As they walk to the classroom, Daniella tries to explain that the things she is asking for the Halloween celebration has always been part of the rules for any party at school.

"Hmph! Well I guess you have a point but I don't like being told what to do!"

Ms. Foley stomps off.

The day went by with only the usual upsets and challenges and Daniella had already made a mental note to get copies of her resume made. She still had not done so but was definitely done with this school and Mr. Griggs.

After school Daniella stopped at the store to pick up some items for that night's potluck

Monday morning, Daniella was walking from her car to the school building when she spotted Ms. Foley before the lady saw her.

Once again the usual conversation started with Mrs. Foley demanding Daniella do things for her child that were outside of her job. Daniella gave the usual answers and excused herself before she said something she regretted.

As the day begins, Daniella has to put the conversation out of her head and deal with the usual challenges of working at a school with no leadership. Halloween is day after tomorrow and there is much to do before the chaos ensues.

On Halloween as Daniella is cleaning up from the class party, she is thinking about when she was in college and she thought she would enjoy these kinds of activities. Maybe it was just this school she doesn't enjoy.

Suddenly as Daniella was just about finished there was a knock on the door. Daniella opened it to see Mrs. Foley and Josiah. "Hello, she greeted them. I was just finishing up to leave. Everything okay?"

"No! My Josiah says everyone else got more candy then him. Why?"

"No ma'm. Everyone received exactly the same amount. I had premade bags to ensure that."

"He needs more candy!"

"I am sorry, I do not have more candy. I gave everyone the same amount and it's all gone."

"We will see what Mr. Griggs has to say! Remember what I warned you about. You are going to end up hurt if this keeps happening!" With that she stormed off.

November

T HE NEXT DAY was November 1 and as Daniella
headed in to school she was admiring the fact that
she had made it this long.

The morning was passing by somewhat routinely
until she heard a key in the lock during the morning
circle reading time. She was mid-way through the
story when Mr. Griggs walked in. He interrupted the
story and said, "Miss Ellis, we need to talk about how
you give out treats at parties. You have to be fair to all
students. You will have to pay for the extra candy I had
to buy for Mrs. Foley."

"First and foremost this is an inappropriate place and time for this conversation. Two you are way out of line and three I am not paying you for a decision you made. I will see you later. Now kindly exit my room or sit quietly while I finish the story. I don't care which you do just do it quietly."

She doesn't know why she had gotten so forceful, but she has had enough of him. As she returns to the story, she notes that it is the first time all year her class is perfectly silent.

Mr. Griggs watched her for a moment then left.

Daniella finished the story and let out a breath of relief. That man! She continued on with her morning. Then while she was monitoring recess time, she took out her phone and sent a quick text to the union rep. She told him she was sending out her resume and he asked her to wait. He was working on something but it might not happen until right before the winter break in December. She replied she would wait until that break then she would send out her resume.

It's the second week of November and Joshua is looking forward to the week off next week for

Thanksgiving. *I really need this week off,* thinks Joshua. *This is not what I signed up for.*

It's mid-morning and Joshua has just finished his lesson on fractions, and Angelo walks in. He looks slightly disheveled with a bloody lip and slips quietly into his seat. Joshua walks over to him.

"Angelo, are you okay? It looks like your lip is bleeding."

"I'm fine! Leave me alone!" His outburst is startling, but Joshua decides that this might be best.

Later during lunch, Angelo comes up to Joshua. "Mr. Shaw?"

"Yes Angelo?"

"I'm sorry. I got jumped on the way to school and yeah."

"I'm sorry, do you want to call home?"

"No, my mom knows, I called her from the office."

"I'm glad you told me. Would you like to talk about a plan to keep you safe?"

"Nah, I'm good. My mom and me are talking about it tonight."

"Good. Do you need anything from me?"

"Nah. I just wanted to say I'm sorry."

"I get it. Thank you."

"Bye." Angelo walks off and Joshua watches him go. This is out of character for Angelo as he is usually not a student who would apologize or even confide in Joshua. Once he is out of sight, Joshua picks up the phone and calls Angelo's mom.

Two days later, Joshua has brought his class in, had them put their backpacks in the coat area and is teaching math. He looks up and Angelo has gone into the coat area. *He is taking too long,* thinks Joshua. *I better check on him.*

Joshua walks toward the coat area and arrives just in time to see Angelo come out with a gun pointed at one of the boys who has bullied him all year. Joshua lets out a slow breath and steps in front of Angelo. With a calm voice, he says quietly, "Angelo, please hand that to me."

"No! He deserves to die!"

"Angelo, you know who always dies? The one with the gun. Come on and hand it to me. Let me help."

"You can't!"

"Yes I can. Hand me the gun."

"I don't want to shoot you Mr. Shaw!"

"Then don't. Hand me the gun."

Angelo seems to think about things and then hands over the gun. Then he starts crying. Joshua thinks quickly and without turning around he says, "Rows 1 and 2 please go to Mrs. Troy's room. Rows 3 and 4 please go to Mrs. Bryant's room. Rows 5 and 6 please go to Mr. Brown's room."

Once the classroom had been cleared, Joshua removed the bullets from the gun and walked the student to the office. In the office Joshua handed the gun and the bullets to Mr. Griggs. He took them and said that he would handle things from here.

After school, Joshua went to see Mr. Griggs. "Mr. Griggs, I wanted to follow up with you and give my statement. I typed it up today while kids were at computers. I think I got it all but I wanted to be sure to write it down while it was fresh in my mind."

"That's alright. I don't need a statement."

"That's unusual. Don't the police usually want to talk directly to the people involved?"

"I didn't call the police. I gave the items back to the parents. This is fourth grade. Don't overreact. I reminded the parents that toys at school of this nature are inappropriate."

"What?!" Joshua asked incredulously. As he walked away, Joshua knew what he had to do. When he reached his classroom, his first call was to the union rep. Next he called the police and made a report. Then he called District office and gave them the police report number.

The next morning, Mr. Griggs came to see him before school. "Mr. Shaw, I need you to sign this." He thrust a piece of paper towards Joshua. Joshua took it and read it. He looked up at Mr. Griggs.

"How do you look yourself in the mirror? No, I am not signing this pack of lies."

"You have to sign it."

"No I do not."

"Then I am placing you on administrative leave."

"You cannot do that without my union rep present."

"It's already done. Go home until the investigation is finished."

Joshua picked up his phone and called his union rep. Just then a sub walked in. "Mr. Shaw, this is your sub for the day. Please be kind and show her what you planned for today." With this, he turned and walked out as if he hadn't a care in the world.

Joshua looked at the sub and sighed deeply. She looked at him and acted a bit uncomfortable. "Listen I uh, well that was …., um things seem bad here. I'm sorry."

"It's not your fault. It's his." Joshua motions towards the door. By the time Joshua had finished showing the sub the plans for the day, the union rep had arrived. The two of them shook hands and headed to the office.

In the office Mr. Griggs had the school resource officer. He looked up to see Joshua and Ramon at the door. "Ah just in time. I was just telling Officer Marsh that Mr. Shaw just doesn't understand the climate here at the school."

The officer stood up and stretched out his hand and shook Mr. Griggs hand and said, "Thank you Mr. Griggs for straightening that up. Gentlemen." He nodded at Joshua and Ramon and started through the outer office.

"Hold it a minute sir." Ramon called out. "You have not done a full investigation. You must do that before you close the case."

"Careful now, things don't work the same way for the police as they do for schools."

The officer then strode out of the office before anyone could stop him.

Ramon cast a glance at Joshua and then told Mr. Griggs that they needed to meet with him immediately.

"You need to make an appointment, I need to be out for supervision during recess. I can't meet with you right now."

"That's okay," replied Ramon, "We will just go over to the district office."

"Fine, I can give you three minutes."

The three men walk into the inner office. Ramon hands Mr. Griggs a list of complaints that the union is filing against him. He reads the paper and tosses it on the table.

"Anything else?"

"You don't want to discuss this situation?" Ramon asks.

"There is nothing to discuss. Anything else you want to say?"

"You need to reinstate Mr. Shaw and tear up the Administrative leave forms immediately."

"Too late, I sent them to the district office last night. Mr. Shaw is on administrative leave until the investigation is complete. I hope that it will come out in his favor but I had no choice to but to report his actions to the district for review. Now I need to go. Good day."

Mr. Griggs gets up and leaves the office without even a look back. Ramon and Joshua look at each other. Ramon says, "Let's go outside."

Outside Ramon says, "Let's go to the district office. I am going to help you with the formal complaint. Then we need to go to the precinct office and make a formal complaint against officer Marsh. Then we need to hire you a lawyer."

The day was completely taken up with filing complaints and writing statements. By 2 o'clock, Joshua was exhausted and hungry so he thanked Ramon and then went home, ate some lunch and began searching for a lawyer. He also wrote his resignation letter. Fortunately, he had some savings and he lived alone in a small apartment so he didn't need much. He could take time off without too much trouble. He decided though that he would not resign until his name had been cleared. This principal really was too much.

On the Friday before the break, Mr. Griggs made an announcement over the PA for staff to not forget the holiday feast in the library after school. When the staff arrived, Daniella noticed that the "feast" was crackers, cheese and apple cider. Good thing she had already invited all the teachers over to her house that night! Then they would get to see a real feast! Of course it was potluck style but Daniella had made sure that there would be plenty of food. It was great to see how the staff was bonding this year. Maybe they could have a good year as a staff even though the school itself has so many issues.

The Thanksgiving week went so fast and before she knew it Daniella was already on her way back to school Monday morning. This was the last week of November and there was so much to do. Well four short weeks and they will be on Christmas break. Everyone had heard about the gun threat and nerves were frayed.

The Thanksgiving break helped but everyone was still jumpy. Daniella had decided that she was going to keep her door locked and shut. Oh wait, she already did that. The other thing that she decided was that she would take some personal time off. She decided she was going to go her doctor and get a doctor's note for some time off. She is really tired of everything at the school and now that there was a valid gun threat and Mr. Griggs did not take it seriously, she really felt in danger.

It took about a week but Joshua was finally reinstated and the administrative leave rescinded. He came back to school a week after the Thanksgiving break. It was chaotic but Joshua was relieved to be back.

December

ECEMBER IS SUCH a short month for schools but yet so much was happening. There were more fights this month than all the months leading up to now. There were almost three fights a day in Daniella's class and she had redone her seating chart four times in two weeks. She finally came to the conclusion that maybe her students just needed some community building time so she was trying to incorporate more games into her lessons.

Finally she got to a point during the second week of December where she just didn't feel good and decided to use a sick day. Her first sick day of the year to be exact. She called off the second Tuesday of the month and spent the day in bed fighting what appears to be the flu. She hadn't had a chance to go to the doctor yet, but if she didn't fell better tomorrow, perhaps she could go then.

The next day she didn't feel great but she went back to work anyways. The kids for the most part seemed to actually feel bad that she didn't feel good and seemed to try to be good. Mr. Griggs however, was beside himself.

"Ms. Ellis, you really put the school in a bad position when you call off. We had no one to sub for you and had to put the kids in separate classes. If you keep calling in sick we will have to discuss your position here."

Daniella doesn't quite know what made her do it. Maybe it was the fact that she was sick. Maybe she was tired. Maybe she was just sick and tired of all that had happened. Maybe she was more spooked than she realized by the gun threat. All she knows is that she suddenly lost her mind.

"Mr. Griggs, you need to stop this immediately! I have called in sick once this year. You are a bully and not a nice person! You need to leave me alone or you will regret it!" She gave her hair a flip and walked away to the ladies restroom. It was the one place she knew she could go and not be followed.

As she walked into the restroom, she started to shake. *Oh my God! What did I just do! I lost my temper on my boss! What was I thinking!!!* As she slowly starts to breathe and stops shaking, she washes her face and comes out. Mr. Griggs is nowhere in sight so Daniella goes to her classroom and starts her day.

As the end of the day approaches, Daniella packs her bag to take home and finishes the lessons for the day. As the day winds down, she tries to calmly wait for students to be picked up but all she can think about is going home and laying on the couch until her husband gets home. When the last student is picked up she spends about ten minutes to finish cleaning up the room and then grabs her bag and heads to the side entrance to the school.

As she exits the building she runs into Joshua. "Hi Joshua."

"Hello."

"Are you alright?"

"Yes. Did you know that I am planning on leaving? I have put in my resignation effective the last school day before the Christmas break."

"I heard you were leaving but I thought it was at the end of the year."

"No, I cannot work for a principal like Mr. Griggs. He did not act like this in the interview. I feel like I got a lot of lip service."

"I know. I am going to send out a bunch of resumes myself."

"Well good luck." Joshua walks away looking sad.

Daniella heads home to rest.

———

One week later, it is Wednesday and Joshua receives a call from the office during the beginning of the Math lesson that Jonathan wouldn't be in class the rest of the week because his sister was killed the night before. Police were still looking for the shooter. Since this is the last week before break, he will return the first week in January. Joshua feels like he has been punched in the gut. She was only a Kindergartener! He composes himself and goes on with his teaching. At the end of the day, Joshua sits down at his desk and feels the heaviness in his shoulders as he hunches over his desk. Usually Joshua has perfect posture, but today, it seems he has forgotten how to hold his posture.

He writes a short note to Jonathan's family to express his condolences and then packs his things and leaves the school. He goes to the post office to mail the letter and then goes home. Once home, he takes out a bottle of wine and pours himself a glass.

The next morning Joshua is trying to do a fun project with his students but he finds himself feeling down. He just can't seem to pull himself out of this sadness although he is faking it well enough for his students. He has not told them that he is leaving, he is saving that for tomorrow, but he is sad that he will not be able to say goodbye to Jonathan and express how sorry he is for his loss.

The day goes by quickly with Joshua spending most of it in a fog. Even when Daniella comes by to check on him after she heard about Jonathan's sister. The announcement was made over the PA today but it was weird. Mr. Griggs simply said, "This week one of our students died. We are sad but we honor her by being happy. So let's be happy." He didn't announce her name or anything. It was the strangest announcement he had ever heard after an event like this.

The next day at the end of the day, Joshua announced to his class that he would not be returning after the holidays. He gave them each a small gift that reflected their personalities and a notebook that the first page of each one had a special note to each of them.

He knew he would miss all of his students and they had already had one teacher leave and now another one that he really felt like he was betraying them, however, this was something he had to do. He prayed that everything would work out in the end.

His students were visibly upset but they seemed to take it well and left the classroom seemingly happy for the holidays although he knew that some of them were not going to happy homes.

Meanwhile, Daniella over in the lower primary hall was saying goodbye to her students for the break and was pleasantly surprised when one of the girls ran back to give her a hug. She wished them a happy holiday season and then closed her door to clean up her room before leaving for the holidays.

Daniella did not take long to clean up and leave, but she did make sure that she called her union rep to wish him a happy holiday as well.

Within 30 minutes of school getting out for the day everyone had left the building except the principal........

The Principal

MR. GRIGGS WAS in his office when he suddenly realized how quiet it was. He decided to walk the grounds. He started on the upper floors where the upper grades classrooms were. He walked through checking each classroom realizing that everyone had gone. Then he checked the lower primary grades hallway to find that they were just as empty.

He had let the office staff go early so now he thought that maybe he should lock up the school. He walked the grounds and locked all the gates and doors then returned to his office. Janitors wouldn't come tonight. They won't return until the Sunday night before school resumes so it should be a quiet night to work late. Mr.

Griggs had no family to go home to, he had no extended family to spend the holidays with since both of his parents had passed away several years ago. It was just him and a tv dinner so why not just stay here and get some work done.

About an hour had passed when Mr. Griggs sat back from his computer and stretched. He suddenly thought he heard a sound in the hallway but then thought he couldn't have because the school was empty except for him. It was probably outside. *Maybe it was a ghost,* he chuckled out loud to himself.

Soon he was engrossed in his work again and forgot about the noise. About another half hour passed when he needed to stretch. He stood up and stretched and walked to the other side of his desk and stopped at the table in the center of the room. He was looking at a requisition form when suddenly the office door flew open. He stood up and saw a figure in the doorway. There the figure stood, gun raised right at Mr. Griggs head.

"Wh-wh-what are you doing here? How did you get in? Hey, wait……." These were the last words that Mr. Griggs would ever utter. The sound of the gun would be the last thing he ever heard. As the bullet sailed through the air into his head, he fell and laid prostrate on the floor. The assailant was so full of rage that he then grabbed the group of pencils off of the desk and began stabbing Mr. Griggs' body over and over again in the stomach and upper body until the pencils broke off. "Take that! Maybe YOU can learn something!" Then the assailant threw the pencils on the floor and stormed out. Mr. Griggs just didn't learn how to be a good principal. Now he has answered for his evil deeds.

The Discovery

IT'S 5:55 AM, the day after the holiday break and Jeff Brinkman slowly starts to unlock the doors of the school. As he walks over to the alarm panel, he finds it strange that the alarm is not beeping. Then he sees that the alarm is not set. *I bet that Mr. Griggs forgot again. He forgets to set the alarm so often, it's a wonder that the general public hasn't found out and broken in a number of times,* Jeff thinks to himself. *Yep, he forgot again. I will talk to him one more time before I start reporting this.*

Jeff goes around and starts turning on hallway lights and unlocking main doors. It's 6:30 before he gets a chance to make his way towards the prinicipal's office. There is a no light coming from under the door but sometimes he doesn't turn on the light. He knocks but there is no answer. *Hmm...there is no answer. Now that is unsual. Mr. Griggs always answers, even if he is on the phone. Maybe he went to the bathroom or something. Or maybe he's just not her yet. Well I will talk with him later.* He walks away and goes back to work on his morning routine.

Veronica bustles in through the office door and hurries to her desk just outside of Mr. Griggs office. She is a bit flustered today because she usually comes in early about 7:00 so that she has an hour before school starts to listen to messages, the absences of students and get the list of subs organized for the day. However, today she is running really late since it is almost 7:30. She notices that Mr. Griggs door is cracked. The light is not on and he doesn't call out. Nothing strange about that. He often didn't say hello when she came in. She would go in and apologize in a minute. She put her things down, took a calming breath and turned on her computer. Then she turned and walked over to the inner office door and knocked.

There was no answer so she gently pushed the door open. For a moment she stared in stunned silence at the bloody body on the floor. Then she started screaming. Her screams brought several teachers from nearby classrooms and the few who were signing in on the roster in the office.

There are various responses from the teachers including gasps and startled surprise. It was the custodian who had appeared when he heard Veronica screaming, that said, "No one touch anything! I am calling the police!"

Everyone moved to the outer office. Who was in charge? Teacher in charge when Mr. Griggs had to be off campus used to be Madelyn. Who was it now? There was no one. Daniella felt that some direction had to be given.

"Okay everyone. Kids are beginning to arrive so I suggest that we open our doors, gather kids in our rooms and wait for further instructions from either the police or the district. I will call the district right now."

The teachers slowly split up and went to the playground and hallways to gather children who were arriving. Daniella called the district office and said to keep all the kids in their classrooms, they were sending someone.

Daniella made the announcement over the PA to the teachers to keep everyone inside for now, then she went to her own room.

By the time Daniella was finished, the police had arrived and were beginning their work. The custodian led them to the body past Ms. Veronica who was still very freaked out and not able to focus on her work. The officer walked into the inner office and then reached for the clip on his shoulder hooked to his radio.

"Dispatch, this is officer Davis. I'm at Brookfield Elementary and I am going to need more of a presence here and I need homicide detectives please."

About ten minutes later, two homicide detectives walked in. They took the officers outside and asked them to not bring anyone to the school just yet. They would evacuate the school . The detectives were to act as if they were brought in to help with the release of the students.

Just then the district representative walked in. He presented himself to the office staff and asked who was in charge. Veronica who looked very shaky pointed at the Homicide detectives.

"Hello officer. I am Dwayne Hays from the district office." Looking at Veronica, " Is there a room nearby we could use?"

"ummmmmm........." Veronica is in her chair and seems very distracted and starting off into the distance.

"Miss....." Dwayne walks over and taps her shoulder.

She lets out a yelp, and then "OH! I am so sorry! What were you saying?"

"Is there a room we can use?"

"Oh yes, here is a key and you can use the empty classroom down the hall. It's number 18 on your left."

"Thank you." The two detectives and the district representative walk down to the classroom in silence.

When they reached the classroom, the detectives take two close seats and the district representative sits across from them.

"Hello, I am Officer Bryant and this is my partner Officer Spinoza. The first thing I think we need to do is to close the school and send the students home. Please keep details vague at this point to help us with the investigation. Right now if you could simply say that there was a situation that caused the school to close for the week, but that no students were harmed, we would appreciate it. We will help you get students picked up. Please keep teachers here and have them gather in one room so we can tell them what is going on. Do you have any questions for us?"

"Lots. I am not sure what is going on. I was just told to get over here immediately and take over. I am not sure why. What can you tell me at this point?"

"Sure. I can tell you that there was a body discovered this morning and it appears to be the principal of this school. We are not sure at this point when he died or how but it is suspicious circumstances and we must investigate."

"Oh sweet Jesus!" Dwayne exhales slowly. "Yes of course, we must send the students home, I will do anything else I can that you need."

"Thank you. For now let's get the students sent home and the teachers and staff in the library."

The men all stand up and return to the office.

Dwayne goes over to Veronica. "I'm sorry, I need your help. Can you help me send a message on the autodialer to all the parents?"

"Y-y-yes." For the next several minutes the two are busy and finally get the message sent out. Then Dwayne asks for Veronica to help him make an announcement over the PA to the school.

"Hello Teachers, please pardon this interruption. All teachers please bring your classes to the gymnasium with their belongings. Thank you."

Dwayne then talks to Veronica. "Soon parents will get the robo messages and begin arriving. Please just tell them you don't know much and that we are sending students home. Please do not tell them about Mr. Griggs. It would impede the police investigation. Any questions, please refer them to me. Okay? Thanks."

Veronica nods and then begins the emergency procedures to shut down the school. She reaches for the phone to call the cafeteria.

Dwayne walks to the gym as kids are arriving and sitting with their classes. Once all the classes have arrived, he begins.

He claps his hands in a rhythmic 2 single claps and 3 quick claps. The kids copy and look at him. "Hello everyone! Okay, Okay, let's settle down so I can tell you what is going on." The kids finally start to settle down.

"Let me start by telling you what a great looking group you are! I look forward to seeing you more! My name is Mr. Hays. I need to tell you something very important so I want you all to put on your listening ears and make sure they are tight so they don't fall off!" The kids all make motions of tightening their ears.

"Have you ever had a situation where it's not an emergency to call 911 but you have to stop what you are doing and work on that situation right away?" Kids start nodding. "Well we have a situation like that this morning. So while we are sure you are all safe, what we are going to do is send you home for a few more days while we check some things out and maybe fix a few broken things. Would that be okay?"

The room suddenly exploded with noise as the kids realize they have a few days more of vacation. The teachers try desperately to quiet them.

Dwayne then puts the microphone back up to his face and whispers into it., "just one more thing please......" Then he claps the sequence again and the kids settle back down. "Here is what we are going to do. Teachers, Ms. Veronica is bringing in your rolls sheets now. As children are picked up, please cross them off the list. Anyone not picked up within the hour, we will start calling. Teachers, when all of your students have been picked up, please proceed to the library. Thank you."

Dwayne then started a movie for the kids to watch on the big pulldown screen. Fifteen minutes later parents started arriving. Dwayne and the officers helped field questions and sent parents and students home.

Two hours later all students had been picked up and Dwayne headed to the office. "Veronica, please have all teachers and staff report to the library, including yourself."

He then walked to the library. As he walked down the hall, he was joined by the officers. He let out a slow breath.

Detective Spinoza asked him, "You alright?"

"Yes, I have just never had to do any of this before." He runs a hand through his salt and pepper hair. "I never want another day like this."

"We will be right here to help you tell the staff." The detectives exchanged glances unbeknownst to Dwayne. They would be looking for any unusual reactions among the staff.

"Thank you." Dwayne replied. "I appreciate you coming to this meeting with me."

As Dwayne entered the library most of the staff was already there. Dwayne asked them all to take their seats as the rest of the staff straggled in.

"Hello everyone, thanks for all you have done today to help us get students safely dismissed. Now, I have some sad news. Mr. Griggs has died. He was found this morning in his office which is why we sent students home. It........."

Officer Bryant interrupted, "Hello, I am officer Bryant. Mr. Griggs died under suspicious circumstances and we need to investigate what happened. If anyone has any information, my partner, Officer Spinoza is passing around cards with our direct phone numbers on them so that you can call us and we can talk. We have talked with Mr. Hays and we all agree that school will remained closed for the balance of the week to allow us to finish our investigation. We will be interviewing each one of you so please make sure to check this list we received from the office for your current home address and phone numbers. Thank you."

Dwayne started speaking again. "Everyone is released for the day. Please make yourself available to the officers when you are called. We will start school again next week. Thank you."

Everyone slowly got up and started out the door. Daniella was still numb. It didn't feel real. She went to her room and was gathering her things when there was a knock on the door. She opened it to find the two officers standing there. She invited them in.

Officer Spinoza took the lead. As they both came inside, Daniella shut the door.

Officer Spinoza started first. "I was thinking that since you were one of the first people to find the body, we could start with you if that is okay?" The end was more of a question.

"Of course," Daniella replied. "I will be happy to help any way I can."

"You were not the first to find the body, is that correct?"

"Yes that is correct. Virginia found him, and I ran over when I heard her screaming."

"Can you describe what you saw?"

"Yes, I saw him lying on the floor and blood everywhere…..and something sticking out of him… and he didn't look like he was breathing…." While Daniella was talking she became more hurried and choppy in her speech.

Detective Bryant spoke, "Just breathe, you are doing fine. I know this is hard."

Daniella nodded.

Detective Bryant asked, "How did you and Mr. Griggs get along?"

Daniella swallowed hard, but she believed in always being truthful, so she answered truthfully. "Mr. Griggs and I did not get along well. He would tell me things like I was trying to make things too hard or I was reading into situations when I was simply trying to do what I understood his instructions to be, he thought I was controlling and stuck up. I did not like working for him. I believe him to be the cause of many of the problems at this school. However, as much as I did not like working for him, I did not wish him dead."

"Did you ever think of moving to another school?" asked officer Spinoza.

"Yes I did, and I put in multiple requests. My union rep has a copy of them all."

"Were you the only one that didn't get along with Mr. Griggs?" asked Detective Bryant.

"No, most of the staff didn't like him. There has been a high rotation of teachers here since I came and I heard it was like that since Mr. Griggs came to this school."

"How did you perceive his relationship with students and parents?" asked officer Bryant.

"They all loved him, but he always gave them exactly what they wanted."

"Can you give me an example?"

"Yes, I had a parent demanding field trips and daily class snacks for my classroom. Mr, Griggs had said no field trips before October 1. It takes at least two weeks to organize them, fill in all the forms, etc. This parent was yelling at the principal and he came in here and said don't worry about all the required forms, just get permission slips and go somewhere within two weeks. He also left several snack items in my room the next day after trying to tell me I had to buy snacks."

"So would you say he undermined you with the parents and students?"

"Absolutely, yes."

"What about his interactions with students?"

"He was overly easy with them. One example is a student who started a fight with another student and caused the other student to need stitches. Mr. Griggs let the student who started the fight order pizza with the school credit card and eat it in the library where he stayed the rest of the day."

"Ok, I think that is all for now. I will have more questions for you in a couple of days. Can I get your phone number?" As officer Spinoza said this and took her number, Officer Bryant was looking around her room at the posters and art work.

They said their good buys and left. Daniella headed home still thinking about everything that had happened.

The Investigation Begins

ON THURSDAY, DANIELLA is sitting at her kitchen table working on some ideas for her classroom for when everyone returns when her doorbell rings. She answers it and it is Detective Spinoza and Detective Bryant.

Officer Bryant says, "Hello Ma'm. May we come in?"

"Of course." Daniella steps sideways to allow them to enter. She moves some things off the table and motions to the chairs near the officers.

"We have a few more questions."

"Of course I am happy to help if I can."

"Have you ever been angry with Mr. Griggs?"

"Yes. Several times."

"What did you typically do when you were angry?"

"I yelled at him mostly. Several times I filed a transfer request. He never forwarded them I found out. I finally this year got my union rep involved."

"How often would you yell at Mr. Griggs?"

"Probably at least once a week. He would make me really mad."

"Have you ever hit him or thrown anything at him?"

"No! Never!"

"So on or about October 31 you did not throw a book at him?"

"No! I threw a book at the wall after he left and one of my students just happened to walk in at that moment."

"On or about September 6th of this year did you say 'I swear I should kill that man!' ?"

"Yes, in my room. Mr. Griggs had just left and he had told me to use my home computer for work, spend my own money for snacks and to get them that night, and to not worry about district rules about field trip but to plan and execute one immediately within the week. I was angry. I really was not meaning harm on him. I just wanted him removed as principal. That is the same date I contacted my union rep for support."

Daniella slowly realizes that she is being investigated.

"How long have your worked at this school under Mr. Griggs?"

"This is my fourth school year. Am I a suspect?"

"We are just asking questions right now ma'm."

"Do I need a lawyer?"

"We cannot advise you on that ma'm."

Throughout all the questioning Officer Spinoza has been quiet. He had been looking around. Now he finally spoke. "On December 19th at approximately 8:30pm where were you?"

"I was here. I had just said goodbye to some friends we had over and was putting my kids to bed. Why?"

"Can anyone verify you were here?"

"My kids and my husband and everyone who just left!" Now Daniella is starting to get nervous. "Are you thinking I had something to do with Mr. Griggs getting killed?" Her voice rose slightly and almost a shrill came from her throat.

"One last question, do you or your husband own a weapon?"

"Yes. My husband has a gun locked in a gun cabinet."

"Thank you ma'm." Officer Spinoza stood. He nodded at Officer Bryant who rose and then looked back.

"Thank you for your time Ma'm. We will show ourselves out."

After they left, Daniella called her husband and together they decided to start looking for an attorney.

On Monday morning, the teachers started returning to school at their normal times. There was an uneasiness hanging in the air. The district representative Dwayne, would take over as temporary acting principal.

Once the school bell rang, he walked into the gym and picked up the microphone and addressed the parents gathered there.

"Hello everyone, Thank you for coming this morning. I am Dwayne Hayes, and I am from the school district office. I am an administrator there who usually supports principals around the district in a variety of ways. In about an hour, the autodialer is going to give you the same information I am about to give you now. Sadly over the winter break, the principal, Mr. Griggs passed away. I don't have many details but I will answer the questions I can. We will have grief counselors on campus for the next month in case you or your students need to talk to someone. In the meantime, I will be stepping in as temporary acting principal. I know this is quite a shock. Please know that my door is open to you. Again, thank you for your time this morning."

About two hours into the school day, he called an assembly. As classes filled in he noticed that there was an air of fear and questions in the air. Teachers led their classes to their spots and encouraged students to sit down. Then he took the microphone and began.

"Okay everyone, let's quiet down. I am Mr. Hayes and I have some news for you. Over the holidays, Mr. Griggs passed away. We don't yet have all the details but we are saddened by his loss. Your teachers, the staff and I will help you as much as we can. We will have counselors on site throughout the month for you to talk to if you need support. I will be acting principal for a while and will answer any question I can. I know this news is shocking so I want to give you some time to process this. Your parents were informed this morning after school began. Please know everyone is here to help you. Thank you."

There was a hushed silence as teachers led their classes back to their rooms.

Throughout the day Mr. Hayes fielded a lot of questions from staff, parents and students. At the end of the day, he walked back into the principal's office. After removal of the body, the district had come in and pulled up the carpet, cleaned the floor underneath and areas necessary and put down new carpet. It was amazing how fast all this happened. It looked like a completely new office.

He sat down behind the desk and let out a deep breath. It felt like he had been holding it all day. There was suddenly a knock at the door leading to the hallway. He looked up to see the custodian. He motioned him in.

"um sir…..um…..I guess I should have checked the office earlier, because you see, well….I always checked in with Mr. Griggs when I get in but that morning….. well his light was off and when he didn't answer when I knocked, I figured he must be in the bathroom or not even here yet but that wouldn't have been him…..I'm sorry Ms. Veronica had to find him……."

"You can't blame yourself. That was a logical conclusion. Do you know anything else we can tell police?"

"No, except maybe that the alarm was never set….."

"Good I will relay that information."

"Thank you sir." With that Jeff left to attend to his duties.

Dwayne calls Officer Spinoza and leaves a message to call him back that some new information came about.

Then Dwayne begins to look over the school basics, such as the schedule list of teachers and staff, the population of the school and then the demographics. As he is looking over the demographics, he notices that there were no suspensions, detentions or even office referrals noted for the last four years. He had heard that Mr. Griggs was an exceptional principal, but how did he not have even one office referral? That would be odd for any school but for a school with a little over 700 elementary kids, surely there was at least one fight or something....... He then starts to look at fifth grade files. He is still only about halfway when he sits back to stretch and notices that the clock reads 8pm. Where did the time go? He rises and gathers his belongings and shuts off the light. He then locks the door to the principal's office and then the main office. He then walks to the front door, reaches to set the alarm and then walks out and locks the front door. All the while he is thinking, *Maybe Mr. Griggs was not as good as his reputation at the district suggest.....*"

The next day, Mr. Griggs is walking towards the front of the school when an idea hit him. Instead of constant wondering, he would just ask. Someone on staff must know how Mr. Griggs was able to keep his discipline numbers down.

For now, he will walk around the school today and observe what is happening. Kinda get a feel for the school and how it operates. He unlocks the door and disarms the alarm. He walks to the office and as he is putting his items down in the inner office, he picks up the map so he can begin walking around the campus and get used to where everything is. He felt like he knew most of it having been on campus all week last week, but it couldn't hurt to have the map with him. Besides, he could use it to mark where each teacher was. He grabbed a clipboard from his briefcase and put the map on it. Just as he was about to walk out of the office to begin his self-guided tour, Jeff Brinkman knocked on the door to the hallway. He opened it and said, "Good morning!"

Jeff started for a minute and said, "Good morning. I didn't expect you to open your own door. Usually I just call out Good Morning when Mr. Griggs says hello then I get to work. He insists on knowing I am here on time."

"Well, Good morning. I will assume you are here on time unless I have reason to not think so and I will talk to you in that case. I appreciate being able to say good morning however. So, Good Morning. I was just about to walk the campus. Want to join me?"

"Sure."

As the two walk the campus and unlock the gates, Jeff shares what he can about Mr. Griggs and how he ran things. "He was very confusing. He never seemed to get upset at the kids. Only the teachers. I overheard him from time to time tell teachers they were overreacting to situations. I probably would have too. When it came to the kids, he was so calm. They could be having a fist fight and he would say who wants to go watch a movie in the library? Or Who wants to play on the computers in the computer lab? I don't know it seemed to break things up pretty quick."

Dwayne listened and was trying silently to figure out what the plan was. When the two said goodbye about twenty minutes later Dwayne was more confused than ever. Throughout the day, Dwayne visited classrooms, spoke to teachers when there were no students, spoke to students. By the end of the day, he believed he had his answer. There were no consequences just distractions. Nothing was ever documented about behavior from Mr. Griggs, because it appeared he did not like paperwork. But where did all the referrals from the teachers go? It just didn't make sense. When he returned to his office, he found the answer. All of the referrals were in the individual teacher's personnel files along with writeups on most of the teachers. Did he really have a teacher problem? Not from what he saw today. He will have to be more observant.

The next day, Dwayne was helping to supervise lunch recess when a fight broke out between two fourth graders. He had both boys sent to the office. When he got there after lunch to talk with them, they stood up and one of them said, "Library or computer room?"

"Neither. My office, both of you."

The two boys looked at each other in surprise. Then they followed him to the inner office. The other boy spoke up and said, "If you are ordering pizza I only like pepperoni."

Dwayne looked at them for a hard moment and motioned for them to sit at the round table in the office. "Why do you think I should order you pizza?"

"That is what Mr. Griggs always does, I mean did when we fight."

"You are Dante, right?" The boy nodded. "Well Dante, I do not believe that you should be rewarded for bad choices, do you?" The boy shook his head.

"And you are Angelo, correct?" The boy nodded.

"So who wants to tell me about this fight?" Both boys shifted in their seats and snuck peeks at each other.

It was Dante who spoke first. "I claimed the playground area because he claimed the basketball courts."

"Isn't there room for you both at each of these sites?"

"NO! I'm with the bloods and we don't associate with the devils" Dante was suddenly angry and ready to fight again.

"Hold it!" Dwayne now had both arms stretched out to either side of the round table. "My understanding is that you can only do minor things in the gangs right now. You can't be a part until you are in middle school….isn't that correct?" Both boys nodded.

"So this is all about gang territory, am I right?" Again both boys nodded. "I am told that both gangs have agreed to consider the school as neutral territory. Is this correct?"

"Yes, but he started it!" Angelo is now ready to fight again.

"Do your parents both know that you guys are hanging around the gangs?"

Dante said, "My mom is never home. She don't care."

Angelo responded with "My parents are sad all the time on account my brother got killed by the bloods two years ago."

"I see. I am sorry to hear that Angelo. However, the school is neutral and there is no fighting allowed here. I will be informing each of your parents. This is your one and only warning. No more fighting. Since no one is hurt you two will miss lunch recess tomorrow and will have clean up duty in the cafeteria. Is that understood?" Both boys nodded. Then he went on, "The next time you two are caught fighting, it will be suspension, understood?" Again they nodded.

He then sent them back to class one at a time. He called Dante's mother first. She was at work, so he asked the manager if she could come to the school. Then he called Angelo's parents and reached his father. His father said he would be there soon.

When Angelo's father arrived, Dwayne showed him into the inner office. "Thank you for coming."

"I'm confused why I am here."

"You son was fighting with another student and it seems that he has been hanging around a local gang. Are you aware of this?"

Angelo's father was in total shock. "What?!" "I mean okay, we have been a little preoccupied the last two years since…..since his brother….."

"Forgive me. Since his brother was killed?"

"Yes, how did you know?"

"He told me. I think now the important thing is to devise a plan to help him. Has your family received any grief counseling?"

Angelo's father shook his head. "I don't like talking about my troubles with a total stranger."

"I understand that. It can be quite helpful though. I can arrange for some through the district if you like."

"Thank you. That would help. I had no idea he was hanging around a gang. I will be more watchful and spend more time with him."

"That's good. As for the fight today, he will have cleanup duty at lunch time tomorrow. I have warned him, if he fights again, he will be suspended."

"I understand and I am sorry. Thank you." Angelo's father stood up. The two men shook hands and Angelo's father left.

Then Dwayne brought in Dante's mother.

Before they had even entered the office, she started. "Why am I here? Why did you call my boss to send me here? I am a single mother working two jobs and I cannot afford to lose one of those jobs because you want to talk to me! This better be important because I already know Dante isn't hurt!"

"Thank you for coming in. Dante was in a fight today."

"Okay and? Don't boys fight? I can't come down here every time he has a disagreement with someone."

"Fighting is not allowed at school. So, you might want to impress upon him your position."

"Mr. Griggs never had a problem with fighting."

"Mr. Griggs is not here. I am. There is no fighting allowed here. For the fight he will have cleanup duty in the cafeteria tomorrow instead of recess. If he fights again, he will be suspended."

"That's it? You called me because of a kid's fight?" At this point, Dante's mom is acting a little angry.

"I also wanted to tell you that Dante tells me he has been hanging around a gang lately. Are you aware of this?"

Now Dante's mother has become speechless. "But, but he is home at night with his sister. She is in high school and his brother is in middle school. They are all at home......." Her voice trails off.

"I am sorry. I know this is hard. I can have the district youth support team reach out to you. They can help brainstorm some ideas for support for you and your family. Would that be okay?" She nodded.

As she stood up to leave, she turned back. "I'm sorry. I didn't know....." Then she turned and left. Just then the afternoon bell rang. About 5 minutes later Dwayne is helping guide students out and greeting parents.

About ten minutes later as most students have been picked up, Mrs. Foley approached him. "Mr. Hughes! You have to talk to that crazy teacher! She is giving my baby too much homework and then marking him when he doesn't do it! And she is not giving them snacks in class. She doesn't watch them at lunchtime and my boy gets picked on! She hasn't even had a field trip! She doesn't do her job!

Mr. Hughes said, "Let's step into my office shall we?"

Mrs. Foley follows him with a smug look on her face as if she has already won. When they are seated in his office, he reaches over to his desk and grabs a notepad and pen.

"Okay, let me ask you some questions, so I can make some notes, okay?"

"Yes sir!"

"Please forgive me, what is your name again?"

"I am Mrs. Foley and this is my son, Josiah."

"Who is his teacher?"

"Mizz Ellis"

"Okay so the first issue is homework, correct? Can I see the homework for tonight?"

"Well it's a packet she gave at the beginning of the week."

"I see. And you say there are no snacks in the classroom, is that correct?"

"Yes. My boy has gotta eat."

"Okay and you say Josiah is getting picked on during lunch recess? Is that right?"

"Yes, she is not watching them."

"Okay, anything else?"

"Isn't that enough? She ain't doing her job!"

"Okay, I think I see the issues. I will check in with Mrs. Ellis about the homework and get a clear picture of what her expectations are. So let's table that until tomorrow so I can talk with her. As for snacks, Mrs. Ellis is not required by the district to provide snacks. Let me speak with her and see what her policy is regarding snack time. As for lunchtime. I am out there during lunch time as the teachers are granted 30 minutes duty free by their contracts. Josiah, would you like to tell your mother what I have seen this week with you at lunchtime?"

Josiah shook his head no. Dwayne continued "Well your mother seems to think you are getting picked on at lunchtime. Are you?"

"y-y-yes" Josiah responds.

"You are??" Dwayne asks with mock surprise. "What about what happened with the two little girls in Kindergarten today?"

Josiah looks sheepishly at his mom, "I pulled their hair. Then I pushed one of them down."

"And yesterday?"

"I took Leon's lunch bag and threw it on the roof."

"So are you really getting picked on?"

"No. But they don't want to play with me! They have to play with me!" Josiah is almost whining now.

"And we talked about how to make friends, right?"

Josiah nodded.

"So you see Ms. Foley, I am sad to say Josiah is not getting picked on, he is picking on others. I will follow up on your concerns and will be happy to meet with you first thing in the morning, say 7:45?"

"Hmph!" Mrs. Foley grabs Josiah and heads out the door. She is mumbling something under her breath as she leaves.

Unfortunately, these were not isolated issued with parents. He has been handling issues like this all week. Perhaps this is something that the police might want to know about. He reaches for his phone and dials the number to the investigating officer's desk.

Suspects!

THREE MONTHS HAVE gone by. Except for random visits from the detectives, life has semi returned to normalcy with some notable differences.

Courtney had returned to try again much to Daniella's delight. Open positions throughout the school were now being filled. Joshua had returned and seemed happier.

About a month prior, Daniella was concerned that she, Joshua or Courtney might have been a suspect in Mr. Griggs' murder because the detectives seemed most interested in the three of them. Then suddenly about two weeks ago the questions about them seemed to stop altogether.

The questions then seemed to revolve around students. Particular students in the upper grades. Surely a student didn't do this. Yes, they had students that were out of control and yes there were some rougher students, however, they would have acted impulsively and not have come back at night to do this. Yet Daniella knew enough to let the detectives finish their investigation.

Beginning of April brought the promise of the Spring Break. Everyone was tired but excited to have the coming vacation. The last day before Spring Break arrived and about 4:30 Mr. Hughes leaned back in his chair and stretched a moment. Then he heard a knock on the door.

"Come in." He replied to the knock.

"Mr. Hughes, I am leaving a little late but I just wanted to say Thank you. I am enjoying teaching again and I appreciate the chance to come back and try again." The young woman smiled.

"Thank you Miss Mosely, it is a pleasure to work with you. I hope you have a good break."

"Thank you, you too." With that she turned and left.

Mr. Hughes looked around and thought, *Nothing here that can't wait until we return.* He stood up, put some papers into his briefcase and walked out of his office, closing the door as he left.

School had resumed and by the end of the week, Joshua noticed that Jonathan had not been in school all week. He checked in with the office and knew that the attendance calls had been made with no return phone call. He made a mental note to check in with Mr. Hughes later in the day. Joshua really liked him and appreciated his straight forward attitude.

After lunch, Mr. Hughes came in with one of the third grade teachers. "Mr. Shaw, please forgive me for interrupting. Could Ms. Irvington take your class for a few minutes?"

"Of course. Ms. Irvington, we were just discussing how to find the perimeter of a square. Class start the practice page. Ms. Irvington, if they finish early, they can read silently at their desks."

Joshua walks out with Mr. Hughes.

"Joshua, I have an update on Jonathan but I feel that I want to tell you in private. Let's go to my office."

Once inside, Mr. Hughes offers Joshua a cold water."

Fearing the worst for Jonathan, Joshua declines the water. The two men sit at the conference table. Mr. Hughes breathes out slowly.

"Jonathan has been arrested for the murder of Mr. Griggs."

"wh—at???" Joshua sits in disbelief.

"The detectives figured out that only a student or really short person could have shot Mr. Griggs due to the angle of the bullet hole. When the questioned Jonathan, he broke down and confessed. His parents can't afford an attorney so he will have a public defender. You may be approached by an attorney on either side. If that happens you need to let the district know asap. We want to help you find your way through this. Do you have any questions for me?"

"No, I'm just in shock. I may have some questions later."

"That is fine. I'll be here if you need me. Please do not discuss this with anyone outside of this room or designated district personnel, okay?"

"Of course."

"Do you need some time before returning to class?"

"No, I'll be alright. Do we have any idea of why he did it?"

Mr. Hughes takes a deep breath. "He blames Mr. Griggs for his sister's death. Says the gang that was bothering him, did a drive by shooting and missed him and shot his sister."

"Oh man. That is heavy load to carry."

"True."

"Thank you sir. I need to get back to my class but I thank you for telling me personally."

"I'll walk you up and address your class if you are okay with that."

"Of course."

The men head back upstairs. Joshua thanks Ms. Irvington and Mr. Hughes address the class.

"Hello everyone, It is my sad duty to tell you that your classmate Jonathan won't be returning to school for a while."

"Is it true he is in jail?" asked Myron.

"I cannot answer that but I can tell you he will be attending classes elsewhere for a while. A message has already been sent to your parents. Now I will turn class back over to Mr Shaw.

Mr. Hughes left feeling like he couldn't give the answers the kids really needed. Now that automated message was heading out to parents, he would be fielding phone calls the rest of the day.

A Year After The Murder

JONATHAN WAS ARRAIGNED and finally his court date came. Lawyers did indeed call Joshua to testify what kind of student he was but a district and a union rep came with him and it was fine. Meanwhile changes were happening at the school.

Dwayne Hughes has been the biggest change. He is staying through the end of the school year and has had more than a positive influence on the school. The first and perhaps the most important change was in discipline. He is not heavy handed with discipline but tries to get to the root cause and take of the issue at the base of the situation in order to correct the behavior. He still struggled with a few students but overall the atmosphere was shifting. Mr. Hughes decided not only to stay through the end of the year, but he put in to continue permanently and was approved by the district.

The parents were a different story. It took almost a month before he was able to convince some of them he really had their student's best interest in mind. Mostly they did not like the new rules or holding their students accountable for their behavior. Most of the parents did not seem to mind the afterschool homework help or the Saturday classes for parents and students to attend together. It seemed that the most pushback he received was when a decision he made didn't align with what a parent thought should happen. He spent many hours explaining to parents the reasons for things he did. He had initially received some complaints at district from parents as well but now, well those seem to have tapered off.

The teachers were happier too. Teachers no longer came to work wondering if they would be hurt, spit on or the like. Teachers still received disrespect at times and challenging student and parent behaviors, but Mr. Hughes stood behind the teachers and empowered them to do their jobs. Of course, they needed to step up too. So many of them had gotten rather lazy only doing the status quo, but now they had to step up their game a bit. Most of the teachers complied without complaint and began to remember why they liked teaching in the first place. They now planned together both for their own grade and the grades above and below. They had regular meetings and stayed after school on their own time to help students and parents. Classrooms were looking picked up and clean. Teachers actually felt as if they taught that day, which before they felt as if they survived the day. There was still much to do, but teachers felt energized and had actually began brainstorming.

The changes at the school had a positive effect on the community. Several of the parents went back to school to get college degrees. A parent group had been formed to assist the school and now supplies and parent aides were happening in several classrooms around the building.

The community started to take pride in their school and one another and several of the streets around the school were getting cleaned up not only of the trash but the bad influences as well. A neighborhood watch had been started and the middle school and high school nearby have organized groups of students to walk younger kids home that needed support.

Things around the neighborhood aren't perfect, but there is a real change and promise of a better future.

As for Jonathan, the school had not forgotten about him. He was sentenced to 8 years for the killing of Mr. Griggs to be served in Juvenile Detention. Several of the teachers and Mr. Hughes are regular visitors to see Jonathan. Community members and students also visit on a regular basis and support his family. This may have been a tragic story, but something really good has come out of it. Everyone learned how to take care of each other.